"Sometimes you can tell a large story
with a tiny subject."

-- Eliot Porter

UNDERSTORY

jackie bailey labovitz

foreword by
james p. blair

text by
jack sanders

thruthelens editions
Limeton VA
© 2016

Foreword

I have been asked to write a foreword for this wonderful book and I am delighted to do it. Why? Because it gives me an opportunity to tell the backstory of how Jackie Bailey Labovitz's lovely photographs came to be made.

Jackie and I share love for the forest. Because I have had three major assignments from the *National Geographic* to cover the tropical forests of Asia, Africa and South America, and the primary forests of our country she asked me to write this foreword. Since I have had the same kind of experience as Jackie has had, I feel that I can set the scene for you.

It is an early spring morning, the mist is starting to burn off and it looks like there will be little or no wind, the forecast promises no rain and a light overcast...a quick decision has to be made. Yes! Let's forget the other responsibilities of the day, put on the boots, load the gear in the car (camera, lenses, light provisions) and off you go...

I see this scene in each of Jackie's images; the freshness of the early morning light in early spring is almost required to capture the delicacy of each transitory petal. But these plants are only three or four inches high so how does she "get the picture?" Why, on her belly of course! You must always meet your subject face to face. It does not matter if the ground is hard or wet or muddy...nothing else matters, so you set up the camera. Then the wait. You wait for the slight breeze to stop, for that pesky cloud to go away and the sun to rise a little higher so the shadow you don't like moves aside. You wait, you wait, the mosquitos don't matter nor do the no-seeums. The wait is long or short but it doesn't matter because you are all concentration. Now, suddenly you see the picture! You know it will be good and so you click the shutter, Yes. And again, now change the exposure; be sure it will be correct because you have come all this way, hiked across a swamp and scrambled up a steep hill on this day, the best day in the short life of this delicate and ephemeral miracle of life.

This is what Jackie has done for each of the photographs in this book. I admire her dedication, her stamina, and her deep sensitivity to the gifts that nature presents to us each spring. She has been our eyes and her pictures show us something to be surprised by and to marvel at...this combination of beauty, individuality and diversity that if we look carefully at each image we see and really understand what she is showing us. I for one, am very grateful.

James P. Blair
National Geographic
Staff Photographer, Ret.

CONTENTS

Introduction 7

Arranged in approximate blooming order

Bloodroot *Sanguinaria Canadensis* 11

Trout Lily *Erythronium americanum* 13

Round-lobed Hepatica *Hepatica americana* 15

Dwarf Iris *Iris verna* 17

Spring Beauty *Claytonia virginica* 19

Rue-anemone *Thalictrum thalictroides* 21

Virginia Bluebell *Mertensia virginica* 23

Common Blue Violet *Viola sororia* 25

Twinleaf *Jeffersonia diphylla* 27

Dutchman's Breeches *Dicentra cucullaria* 29

Yellow Fumewort *Corydalis flavula* 31

Wild Geranium *Geranium maculatum* 33

Showy Orchis *Orchis spectabilis* 35

Mayapple *Podophyllum peltatum* 37

Mayapple *Podophyllum peltatum* 37

Cut-leaf Toothwort *Cardamine concetanata* 39

Downy Yellow Violet *Viola pubescens* 41

Bird's-foot Violet *Viola pedata* 43

Little Sweet Betsy *Trillium cuneatum* 45

Large-flowered Trillium *Trillium grandiflorum* 47

Large-flowered Trillium *Trillium grandiflorum* 49

Wild Columbine *Aguilegia canadensis* 51

Virginia Spiderwort *Tradescantia virginiana* 53

Pink Lady's-slipper *Cypripedium acaule* 55

Yellow Lady's-slipper *Cypripedium parviflorum* 57

Virginia Waterleaf *Hydrophyllum virginianum* 59

Yellow Stargrass *Hypoxis hirsuta* 61

Blue-eyed Grass *Sisyrinchium angustiflorum* 63

Whorled Loosestrife *Lysimachia quadrifolia* 65

Canada Lily *Lilium canadense* 67

Turk's-cap Lily *Lilium superbum* 69

Spotted Jewelweed *Impatiens capensis* 71

Plant Notes 74

Plant State Index 80

INTRODUCTION

The forest understory — the ground from which the trees grow — is an environment that offers a special challenge to herbaceous plants, both because of the reduced lighting available during most of the season and because of the competition from their much bigger brethren. Lately, that competition has often been increased by enemies above, on and below the ground.

Because the greatest amount of light during the growing season occurs in early spring, most of the flowering herbs in our deciduous understory are early spring ephemerals. They possess a variety of survival techniques, making them among the most interesting of our woodland plants. Over eons, they have evolved methods to take advantage of the short period between the thawing of the ground and the appearance of the leaves on the trees. They arise from the soil and bloom as their leaves are soaking up the sunlight beaming through the barren branches above. Through photosynthesis those leaves use the sun to manufacture food that is sent to the roots and corms. This stored energy will enable the plant to send up new growth the following spring. As the tree leaves appear, the above-ground parts of many of them begin to wither, and by summer, have vanished — which is why they are called "ephemerals."

However, some continue to live through the summer; the Mayapple, for instance, has large spreading leaves that soak up as much of the reduced sunlight as possible. Plants living along the edges of woods and clearings, such as Jewelweed, the Turk's Cap Lily and Canada Lily, have more light and less trouble surviving through a longer season.

While most of the plants pictured here are perennials, they do not live forever and need seeds to assure there will be future generations. Their flowers use many techniques to appeal to insects that provide the pollination needed by most to produce healthy seeds. Attracting insects in the early spring understory is not always easy; it's still cold on many days, and especially nights, and the wealth of insects found in warmer weather is not available. Ephemerals use color, design, shape, and scent to attract the early insects, and nectar and pollen to reward them. Some even employ ants to plant their seeds!

As the season continues and the forest floor becomes "darker," fewer plants produce flowers. While the sun is higher in the sky and consequently stronger, the canopy greatly reduces the light reaching the ground. The plants that have adapted to these conditions often have become specialized in efficiently using light wavelengths that pass through the filtering leaves. Only a few of these will bloom in midsummer, almost always with small flowers. Their blossoms tend to attract flies and other small flying insects of the forest floor instead of bees and butterflies that are more apt to be harvesting in the open sun. Some plants, such as wintergreens, supplement their food generated with chlorophyll by parasitizing or developing cooperative relationships with fungi in the ground.

Some plants wait until fall to bloom. These include woodland sunflowers and asters whose leaves have spent the season slowly gathering the strength needed to produce the flowers. Their seeds are very late in appearing, but most of these autumnal seeds are equipped with "pappi," little tuffs of hair that allow the fall winds to carry them far from the mother plants. They settle in the leaf mulch and sprout in the spring.

In the past decade or two, astonishing changes have been occurring in our environment, significantly affecting native plant populations in many areas, especially the understory. Many of the flowers shown here are becoming harder to find. One problem is the overpopulation of the White-tailed Deer. In some areas, deer have devastated the understory, consuming not only herbs but also the seedling trees needed to replenish the woods.

A second problem is invasive species such as Japanese barberry and Garlic Mustard that crowd out native species.

Another threat is earthworms. Virtually all of the worms we see are aliens that came with Europeans and the plants they imported. In recent times some worm species have moved into woodlands, devouring the protective leaf mulch on the forest floor. As a result the surface of the understory loses its ability to hold moisture, and is exposed to alien plants and erosion. Some native plants cannot survive in these conditions.

Bloodroot

Sanguinaria canadensis. Bloodroot has found its way onto baskets and into medicine cabinets, but, though beautiful, has not made its way into many gardens. That's probably because its petals are quite delicate — a heavy spring shower can knock them off. Nonetheless, Bloodroot is very protective of its young blossoms. As the plants arise from the ground, the leaves wrap the bud-bearing stems like a baby in a blanket, perhaps to protect them from the cold air and stormy weather. This member of the Poppy family was widely used by American Indians and early American herbalists. They employed its orange-red namesake juice both as a dye and as a treatment for skin afflictions, cramps, vomiting, coughs, croup, and many other ailments. However, both Indians and colonists overlooked its main modern use: In 1983, Viadent toothpaste and mouth rinse went on the market, both containing "sanguinarine," obtained from *Sanguinaria canadensis*. The American Dental Association once called sanguinarine a promising plaque-fighter, and a surgeon general of the U.S. Army Dental Corps described it as "the best thing that's happened since fluoride." Bloodroot itself is becoming hard to find in some parts of the East: Foraging deer have destroyed many colonies.

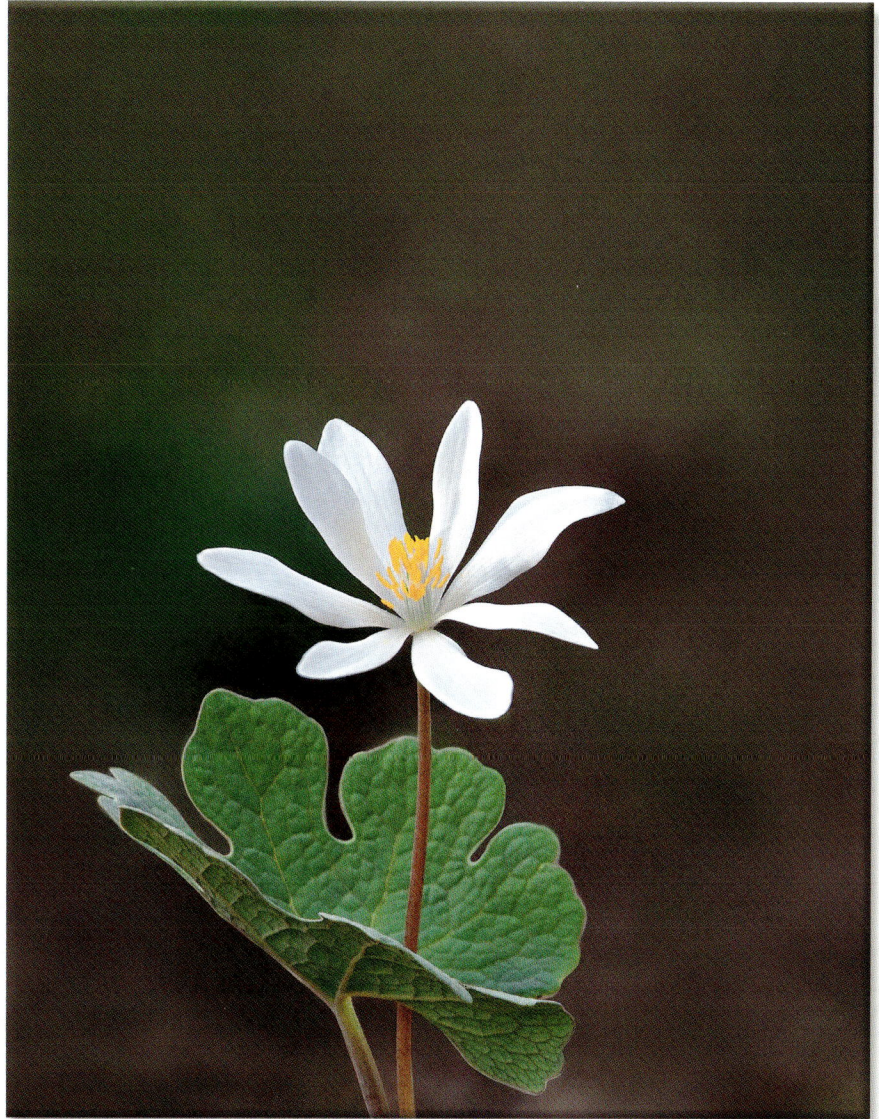

Bloodroot   *Sanguinaria canadensis*

Trout Lily

Erythronium americanum. Despite a vast network of plant parts underground, the Trout Lily offers only a few beautiful blossoms each spring. Trout Lilies form large, sometimes ancient colonies in rich moist soil, often near small woodland streams. Each colony starts with a seed that develops a little corm that grows near the surface and sprouts a leaf. In a year or two, the young corm emits several threadlike "droppers" that burrow down at an angle of about 45 degrees. (Some misguided ones may surface, then dive again — the white "threads" that appear in Trout Lily groves.) At the end of each dropper — several inches lower in the soil and up to 10 inches from the mother — a new corm forms from food sent down the line by the parent. Eventually the link withers away, and the offspring corm sends up a leaf; it makes food to develop a new corm, which in turns sends droppers down even farther the next year. After a few years a sprouted seed may have produced a dozen plants with corms at various depths in the moist earth; after 20 or 30 years, more than a hundred plants form a mat of many mottled leaves. However, only about one percent of the plants in a colony will bloom each year. Some Trout Lily groves can be a century or more old, and their networks of roots, stems and leaves are important in preventing erosion of the forest floor.

Trout Lily   *Erythronium americanum*

Round-lobed Hepatica

Hepatica americana. Early spring flowers can cheer the winter-weary with the first signs of the new season's life, but they can also provide fascinating examples of nature's survival techniques. The beautiful and seemingly delicate Round-lobed Hepatica is just such a survivalist. When the buds, stems and leaves push through the leaves — or even the snow, they bear many little hairs that probably serve two purposes: warmth and defense. Botanists believe hairs help keep frost from the main flesh of the plant. Hairs are also believed to be distasteful to herbivores, especially small mammals that might dine on this early vegetation. Hepatica leaves are long-lasting, remaining through the season but turning a rust color by late in the summer. Over the winter, they shelter the ground for the following season's new growth. In the spring, the old leaves may help warm the ground for that new growth; the rust color is a shade that efficiently absorbs sunlight. The color and shape of the leaf are also responsible for the name of the plant: It's liver-like — hepatica is from the Greek for "liver." Many people believed that because the leaves look like liver, that's a sign from God that they are good for liver ailments, and hepaticas were long used by many cultures as a liver disease treatment and tonic. *Hepatica americana* blossoms may appear in several colors, including white, pink, lavender, purple, and blue, each in a pastel shade that seems too delicate for the harsh weather of early spring. The colors attract early bees, butterflies, flies, and, of course, spring hikers.

Round-lobed Hepatica   *Hepatica americana*

Dwarf Iris

Iris verna. The iris is a fabled flower — and a tabled one, too. The name comes from the Greek goddess Iris, who was a messenger between humans and the gods atop Mount Olympus. Wherever she went, a rainbow followed her. Whenever the ancient Greeks saw a rainbow in the sky, it was a sign that Iris was delivering a message to someone. Thus, iris came to mean "rainbow" and, used as the generic name of these plants, reflects the variety of brilliant colors sported by many species. The Greeks had a more practical use for the iris, however. According to the story, a Greek name for one type of iris was machaironion, and the rhizome of this species was ground with flour to create a variety of pasta. Later this staple became known simply as "macaroni." Among more than 30 Iris species in the United States, Dwarf Iris (*Iris verna*) comes in two versions, Upland, *I. verna smalliana*, which has clumps of flowers, and Coastal, *I. verna verna*, shown here, whose flowers are farther apart in loose colonies. Both employ typical iris techniques to attract large bees: Extremely showy upright displays, which are especially reflective in ultraviolet light; large sepals, which serve as comfortable landing pads; and very effective mechanisms for depositing pollen on the bees seeking the ample quantities of nectar. Perhaps because of destruction of habitat — typically dry oak or pine forests — and theft of plants, the Dwarf Iris is considered endangered in several states. However, since the plant is somewhat poisonous, deer — a deadly threat to many spring natives — appear to ignore this species.

Dwarf Iris   *Iris verna*

Spring Beauty

Claytonia virginica. Being among the first flowers of the season has earned Spring Beauty the affection of many a spring trekker looking for signs of new life in the woods. Spring beauty can colonize and carpet large areas of woodland, painting the brown leaves pink. The flower's five petals glisten in the sunlight, bearing many tiny reflective beacons to catch the eye of the earliest bees and flies, which are guided to the nectar by the several pink lines radiating from the base of each petal. The plants are able to thwart thieves as well as to handle the harshness of frigid nights, fierce winds, and heavy rains common in early spring. Spring Beauty protects its nectar and pollen from crawling insects by using slender stems that many ants cannot easily negotiate. These stems are also quite flexible, able to bend without breaking in strong winds of March and early April. The flower closes when the sun is setting or when rain threatens, helping to conserve heat and prevent rain from diluting the nectar and washing away the pollen. Spring Beauty can also position its slender, grass-like leaves to capture the sunlight arriving at the relatively low angle found in the early spring. Spring Beauty (*Claytonia virginica*) ranges from southern Canada into the mountains of the South and west to the Mississippi River region. Claytonia was named for John Clayton, who came to Virginia as a young man in the early 1700s. A Gloucester County government official for a half-century, Clayton was also a botanist. He spent much of his life collecting specimens, sending them to a Dutch botanist, Jan Frederik Gronovius, who named and categorized them in *Flora Virginica*, published in 1739 and 1743. The Spring Beauty's corm is small, nutlike, and tasty; while it takes time and effort to gather enough to make servings worth eating, fans swear it's worth the trouble.

Spring Beauty   *Claytonia virginica*

Rue-anemone

Thalictrum thalictroides. Unlike many spring ephemerals that use sweets to reward pollinating visitors, the Rue-anemone has no nectar. Instead, it offers only pollen to passing insects. And though it has no scent either, the petal-like white sepals — often tinged with pink, as here — are showy enough to attract bees and flies. The bee is what it wants, for that insect collects the pollen to bring back to the hive — in the process, dropping some grains while visiting other Rue-anemone flowers and thus accomplishing pollination duties. Flies just eat the pollen right there, accomplishing little except fly survival. It and its cousin, the Wood Anemone, are both members of the Buttercup Family (*Ranunculaceae*), many of whose members — including Rue-anemone — contain acrid substances that can blister flesh and cause poisoning if eaten in large enough quantities. This is protection against both browsing mammals and herbivore insects. Perhaps because they bloom amid the early spring breezes, anemones are called windflowers; anemone is from the Greek for "wind." For a long time, scientists called Rue-anemone *Anemonella thalictroides* — literally, "little anemone thalictrum-like." *Thalictrum* is the generic name for meadow-rue, mostly summer-blooming plants with leaves similar to Rue-anemone's. Around 1990, Rue Anemone was reclassified into the *Thalictrum* genus, but the old specific name was retained. Thus, we have the rhythmic, but seemingly silly scientific name, *Thalictrum thalictroides* — "a meadow-rue that's like a meadow-rue." Botanists are still debating this reclassification, so perhaps the name will change again.

Rue-anemone   *Thalictrum thalictroides*

Virginia Bluebell

Mertensia virginica. Unlike so many of the spring forest flowers, Virginia Bluebells have not made a name for themselves as a "practical" plant: They are not edible, and they have little if any history as an American Indian or colonial medicine, flavoring, dye, or other useful herb. Instead, these flowers of rich, moist woods are known chiefly for their beauty. Virginia Bluebells are, in fact, unusually hardy and disease resistant, able to form large colonies of perennial plants with bright blue flowers opening from pink buds. These characteristics have made the species one of the few native spring wildflowers that are popular with gardeners both here and in Europe. Butterfly gardeners are especially fond of the plant because butterflies are the flowers' chief pollinators; the bell-shaped flowers seem shaped by evolution to provide an ideal perch for butterflies while they are drinking the nectar. A flower so colorful and widespread is bound to gain many folk names, and *Mertensia virginica* has been known as Bunchflower, Gentleman's Breeches, and Old-Ladies' Bonnets. It's one of more than 30 *Mertensia* species in North America, and yet it is named for Franz Karl Mertens (1764-1831), a German botanist who specialized in plants of his native land.

Virginia Bluebell   *Mertensia virginica*

Common Blue Violet

Viola sororia. The world of violets is a jumbled one. More than 75 species exist in North America, most of them natives. However, interbreeding has created many new forms and varieties, some of which only the most dedicated scientist could identify. A botanist estimated in the 1940s that about 300 violet species, varieties, and natural hybrids were living north of Mexico. Among the most common is, appropriately, the Common Blue Violet (*Viola sororia*), found in all states east of the Rocky Mountains. In fact, it's so common and spreads so easily that it's often considered a weed. While most violets employ flying insects for pollination, many spring violets also use crawling insects for a different purpose. Ants harvest and "plant" violets and certain other spring wildflowers in a symbiotic relationship called myrmecochory — literally "ant farming." The ants are drawn to the seeds by small protuberances called elaiosomes that contain attractive fats and possibly sugars. The ants carry the seeds, sometimes as far as 70 yards, to their nests where they eat the treat on the outside of the seed. The shell, however, is too hard to open, so the ants discard the seed proper, often in a tunnel in the nest that's used for "trash." Here, amid nutrients provided by the soil and by the housecleaning ants, the seed has a much better chance of producing a plant than one dropped on the forest floor where it might be eaten by foraging birds and rodents. In some environments, myrmecochory also protects the seeds from destruction in wildfires.

Common Blue Violet   *Viola sororia*

Twinleaf

Jeffersonia diphylla. Twinleaf is one of only two species in the genus *Jeffersonia.* Oddly enough, the other lives more than 6,000 miles away in China, Korea and Japan. The genus is one of the few to honor a U.S. president, another being the Washingtonian palm. Thomas Jefferson was considered a naturalist, and the name was selected in his honor by Benjamin Smith Barton (1766-1815), a physician who was also a naturalist, botanist, archaeologist, intellectual, and University of Pennsylvania professor. "Twinleaf" refers not to the fact that it has two leaves, but to the fact that each of its several leaves are deeply divided in two, making each seem like a pair. Possibly the rarest flower in this collection, Twinleaf is protected by laws in at least four states. It favors rich limey woods and can be found high in the mountains bordering the Shenandoah Valley. Earlier Americans knew Twinleaf as Rheumatism Root, so called because it was used to treat the symptoms of that ailment. American Indians have employed the plant for a variety of medicinal purposes, including urinary tract problems, treating sores, and as a tonic. However, like its close cousin, the Mayapple, Twinleaf is poisonous and is better viewed than consumed.

Twinleaf   *Jeffersonia diphylla*

Dutchman's Breeches

Dicentra cucullaria. The name, Dutchman's Breeches, reflects the odd shape of this close cousin of the garden "Bleeding Heart." These are actually four-petaled flowers; two of the petals unite to form the two legs of the pantaloons while the two others are inside, but project like lips over the stamens. The shape has advantages. Each "upside-down" blossom is protected from the effects of rain and wind on the pollen. It's also sealed from invasion by most crawling or small flying insects that might steal the nectar without performing pollination services. In fact, only the long, strong tongue of the female bumblebee is said to be able to consistently reach from the flower's bottom opening up into each of the two, long petal-spurs to lap up the sweets — in the process, picking up and later depositing pollen. Alas, the flowers are not perfect vaults; some wasps, carpenter ants and even bumblebees have learned to chew holes through the tips of the spurs to gain direct access to the nectar. The odd shape of this flower has gained it many folk names — Soldier's Cap, White Hearts, Eardrops, Monk's Head, for instance — but Dutchman's Breeches remains the most common. However, in Victorian times, the name was the subject of controversy and considered "rude" in many circles. After all, breeches were originally underwear, and the early meaning of "breech" was "buttocks" or "rump" — not exactly the stuff of garden club meetings.

Dutchman's Breeches   *Dicentra cucullaria*

Yellow Fumewort

Corydalis flavula. Most early spring ephemerals are perennials, making use of the brief period of pre-leaf light both to bloom and to create and store food for the next year's flowering. Not so the Yellow Fumewort. It's an annual that relies on seeds that sprout the same year they're created — but not until circumstances are just right. Among the earliest of the spring bloomers, *Corydalis flavula* is showing off its small but elegant yellow flowers by April, attracting early insects needed for pollination. By the arrival of summer, seeds have fruited and been dispersed — often with the help of ants that carry them to their nest to dine on the fatty seed appendages called eliasomes. The seeds remain dormant through the period of high summer temperatures that might desiccate the seedlings, and instead wait until late summer and cooler air before sprouting. The seedlings then overwinter and return to life in the spring to become adults. Yellow Fumewort likes a forest floor that is not too deeply covered with leaf litter and, in fact, appears to favor woods that have burned, colonizing spots with little or no litter at all. Burned forest often has less canopy, and fumewort seedlings may take advantage of that in the fall. While American Indians used to burn and breathe in the smoke of fumewort to "clear the head," that's not where the "fume" of the name comes from. The plant is a member of the family called Fumitory, a name from the Latin, *fumus terrae*, "smoke of the earth," because the leaves are grayish. Those fumes the Indians sniffed may have done more than clear the head – Fumitories are members of the Poppy order, famous for their narcotic alkaloids — of which fumitory has several.

Yellow Fumewort   *Corydalis flavula*

Wild Geranium

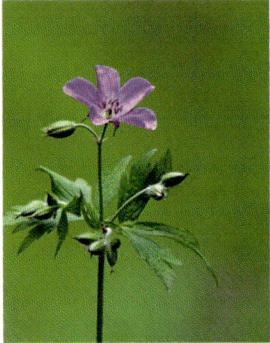

Geranium maculatum. Everyone knows "geraniums," but few know real geraniums. The showy, aromatic plants of gardens and flower boxes are distant cousins from Africa. The real thing grows in our own backyard, the common and widespread Wild Geranium. Geranium means "crane" — the flowers are often called cranesbills. The names refer to the shape of the seed case, which has been likened to the long beak of the namesake bird. When the seeds inside are ripe, the long pod pops and catapults them into the air. The mechanism that propels the fruit consists of the five sides of the beak. As the pods dry, they become tense, stretched springs. When the time is right, they simultaneously uncoil, hurling the seeds up to 30 feet and leaving behind a whorl of curls. Such propulsion helps ensure the spread of the plant into new, but nearby territories, usually with similar soils and the right light. However, when it lands, the seed's trip has not ended. Each has a "tail," called an awn, which curls when it is dry and straightens when wet. Botanists suspect this tail-twisting motion propels the seed very slowly a short distance along the ground until it becomes stuck in a small hole or crevice. At that point, the motion may help push the seed into the soil. This amazing ability to "crawl" into a protected spot may help the seed find a suitable place to eventually germinate while escaping the birds and small mammals that might spot and eat it.

Wild Geranium   *Geranium maculatum*

Showy Orchis

Galearis spectabilis. A denizen of deep woods and ravines, the Showy Orchis is the earliest orchid to appear in eastern North America. It flowers soon after the first bloomers, but in the competition for insect attention, may lose out to other, more plentiful flowers, especially Wild Geranium and the early Iris species that bloom in its neighborhood. The flowers are designed to attract early emerging female bumblebees, and is so finely designed that only the female, and not the later-emerging male, can provide pollination. It does its best to set a fine dinner table, with plenty of food and drink. A pair of pink-to-purple upper petals forms a hood over the reproductive flower parts to protect the rich supply of nectar from the rain. The white lower lip is large and wide, offering a comfortable landing pad for the bee. While the bumblebee is drinking nectar, the flower is slapping pollen onto its hairs, in the expectation that it will be carried to a nearby orchis. The plant was long known as *Orchis spectabilis*, suggesting it was one of the earliest and most basic orchids, but has lately been reclassified as *Galearis spectabilis*. *Galearis* is from the Latin for "helmet," a fitting reference to the protective "hood," while *spectabilis* means "spectacular" or "showy." The plant has also been called Preacher in the Pulpit because the flower parts look like a minister delivering his sermon from an old-fashioned, baffled pulpit.

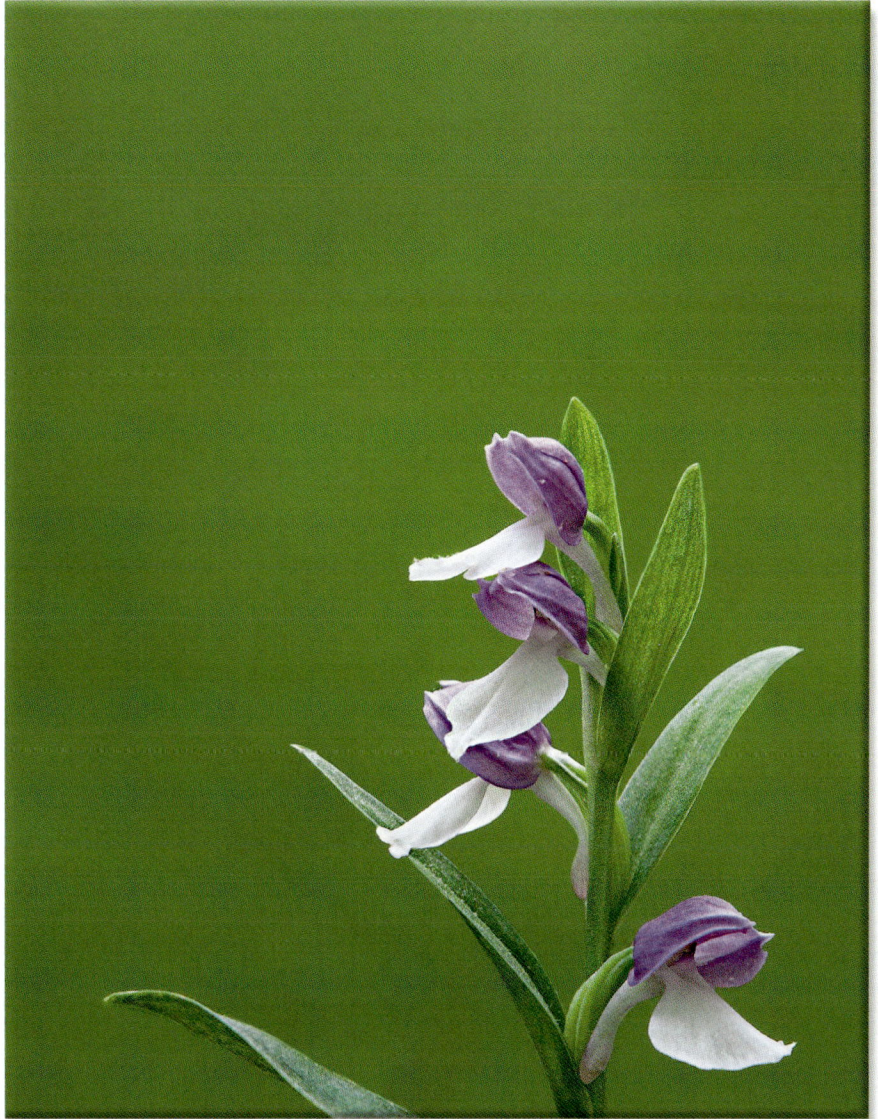

Showy Orchis   *Galearis spectabilis*

Mayapple

Podophyllum peltatum. Years ago, children used to say the "green umbrellas" were out, referring to the colonies of Mayapples, sometimes vast in size, that would unfold their pairs of large leaves in spring. The flowers, which appear from the junction of the two leaves, emit a scent often described as unpleasant; John Burroughs called it "sickly sweet." The fragrance attracts bumblebees, flies and other insects. The flowers have no nectar but do offer plenty of pollen, which bees use for food. Despite the plant's name, the "apple" doesn't appear until midsummer. The large, egg-shaped yellow berry is edible, and farm boys used to relish its taste, variously described as sweet to mawkish to insipid. Captain John Smith tasted Mayapple in Virginia in 1612, describing it as "a fruit that the Inhabitants call Maracocks, which is a pleasant wholesome fruit much like a lemond." Every part of the Mayapple is poisonous — except the ripe fruit; until it is mature, even the berry is poisonous. This is Mayapple's defense mechanism, protecting even the fruit until it's at the appropriate stage of development. Then, for the sake of propagation, the poisonous quality disappears so the berry will be eaten and seeds consumed and "planted." Many mammals, birds, and especially box turtles eat the ripe fruit; one study showed that seeds that had gone through the turtle's digestive tract stood a much better chance of germinating than those that simply fell to the ground. American Indians put Mayapple's poison to use. Menominees and Iroquois turned the plant into an insecticide to kill potato bugs and corn worms on their crops. Among some, it was used to commit suicide. "The root is a very effective poison which the Savages use when they cannot bear their troubles," wrote botanist Michel Sarrazin in 1708.

Mayapple   *Podophyllum peltatum*

Cut-leaf Toothwort

Cardamine concatenata. Generations ago, when we were an agrarian society and closer to the earth, farm children knew about nature's bounty. Walking to school in the early spring, young scholars might pass a wood and spot the white or pink blossoms of the toothwort. They'd pull up some roots and wash them off. They liked the peppery taste, similar to that of the closely related watercress, and would add the roots to sandwiches — or just eat them alone. No surprise, since several species of toothworts are members of the mustard family of flavorful herbs. American Indians knew that, too, of course, but were more sophisticated than farm children. They would ferment the roots for several days, thereby sweetening them. Farm homemakers liked them so much, they'd pickle roots for winter consumption and use them as a flavoring like horseradish. Cut-leaf Toothwort (*Cardamine concatenata*), shown here, is among the earliest of our spring ephemerals, yet a long-lasting one, flowering in March and April, and often well into May. The long blooming season helps guarantee that insects will pollinate their fragrant white, pinkish, or lavender flowers that, like typical mustards, have four petals. However, the toothwort does not need seeds to spread, and can do so via its roots or rhizomes, which can lead to large colonies of these plants. Those roots bear tooth-like projections that give toothworts their common name. The generic name, *Cardamine*, is from the Greek for "heart-strengthening"; it was long believed some European species could treat heart ailments — not, alas, of the lovelorn.

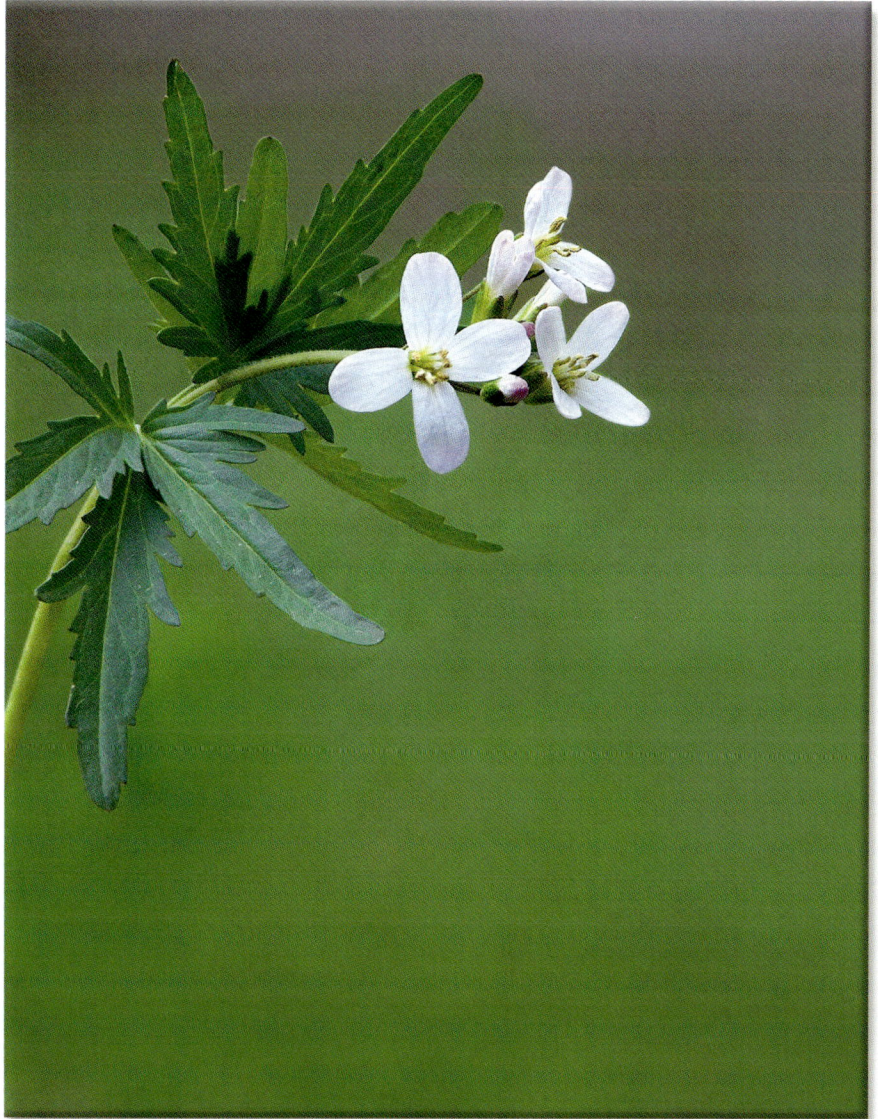

Cut-leaf Toothwort   *Cardamine concatenata*

Downy Yellow Violet

Viola pubescens. Some scientists believe that after green, closely related yellow was the first color developed by flowers as they evolved showiness. Bright colors help to attract insects for pollination. While it seems odd that a flower called "violet" should be "yellow," all yellow violets have at least a tad of blue, purple, or brown, usually in the form of petal lines that are part of their insect guidance system. About a dozen yellow violet species occur in North America. Downy Yellow Violet (*Viola pubescens*) is found in rich, loamy soil throughout eastern and central states. Although it bears beautiful, showy blossoms, few people realize that this and other spring-blooming violets also produce viable flowers that never open. Called cleistogamous flowers, they appear lower on the plant, sometimes under the ground and often later in the season. While they may never open, they nonetheless contain all the necessary parts to produce seeds, though they are not as viable as cross-fertilized seeds. This system may have evolved because so many violets appear early in the season, when insect pollination is chancier than in the warmer, insect-rich months. Not all violets produce cleistogamous flowers. Some summer species, such as Johnny Jump Ups (*Viola tricolor*), bear very colorful blossoms, can easily attract insects, and do not appear to need backups. *Cleistogamous*, incidentally, means "closed marriage." The showy flowers that lure insects are called *chasmogamous*, or "open marriage."

Downy Yellow Violet   *Viola pubescens*

Bird's-foot Violet

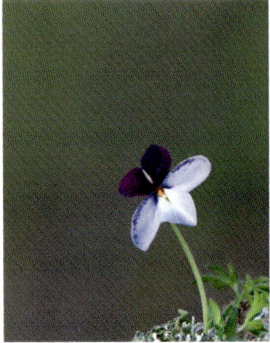

Viola pedata. Few plants are better adapted to life on the forest floor than our violets, and few are better able to use insects to assure their survival. Though small, their flowers are bright, well marked with "bee guides" to direct insects to nectar and pollen, and often well scented to attract the attention of flying passersby. In a way, these plants seem almost smarter than insects. Violet seeds bear sweet, fatty appendages called elaiosomes that attract foraging ants. The ants collect the seeds, carry them to their underground homes, eat the elaiosomes, and then discard the seed itself in their tunnels designed for wastes. Come spring, with its melting snow and its showers, the subterranean seeds, surrounded by other ant detritus that may serve as fertilizer, are moistened and sprout. Thus, using "candy" as payment, violets have employed ants to spread and to plant their seeds. Botanists call this symbiotic process "myrmecochory" — "ant dispersal" or, better, "ant farming." Violets have attracted not only insects, but also an emperor. Napoleon Bonaparte loved violets and the flower became a symbol to his followers, who called him Caporal Violette or Le Père Violet. States, too, like the flower: It's the official flower of Illinois, Rhode Island, Wisconsin, and New Jersey. No other plant genus has been so popular with politicians.

Bird's-foot Violet   *Viola pedata*

Little Sweet Betsy

Trillium cuneatum. The flowers of Little Sweet Betsy bear a color that is found in only a handful of spring woodland ephemerals such as Wild Ginger, Red Trillium, Jack-in-the-Pulpit, and Skunk Cabbage. The maroon red is often accompanied by a distinctive scent that may not always please the human nose. That's because these flowers are pretending to be carrion in an effort, literally, to draw flies. In early spring flies are scouring the forest floor for the freshly thawed remains of creatures that have died over the winter. The flower's color is similar to dead meat, and the scents are often like those given off by carrion — mouth-watering to many kinds of flies. In the case of Sweet Betsy, visitors are typically blowflies or fruit flies. The former, being larger, may be more likely to provide pollen transportation services. However, sexual reproduction in Sweet Betsy is infrequent, and the plant also "clones" itself by underground division of its rootstock, resulting in long-lasting colonies. *Trillium cuneatum*, which favors upland woods, is also called Whip-poor-will Flower, Large Toadshade, Purple Toadshade, and Bloody Butcher. Sweet Betsy refers to its scent, which some liken to banana, and a corruption over the ages of the word "birth." The plant was used in midwifery because it was said to relax the patient, and was consequently sometimes called Birthroot. Birthroot became Bethroot, then just Bet, and finally Betsy. Toadshade, a term used for many trilliums, refers to the large leaves that could, if a toad so wished, provide shade. In chilly early spring, however, any smart toad would be soaking up all the sun it could find.

Little Sweet Betsy   *Trillium cuneatum*

Large-flowered Trillium

Trillium grandiflorum. The great botanist, Linnaeus, created the name "trillium" to describe the "threeness" of the genus, which has three leaves, flowers with three petals, three sepals, three-chambered ovaries, and berries with three ribs. Trilliums are also commonly called Wake-Robins because many members bloom at about the time of the arrival of migrating robins in spring. Large-flowered Trillium, also called White Trillium, is white when young, but often turns pink with age; as shown here. *Trillium* species are found in various shapes and hues throughout much of North America, and some wildflower enthusiasts specialize in growing the more showy white and pink varieties. Large-flowered Trillium is particularly popular because of its large flower; it's the state flower of Ohio and the provincial flower of Ontario. Conservationists report that most of the Large-flowered Trillium plants found in nurseries are probably stolen from the wild. That's because the nurseries can't afford the patience it takes to grow them; it can take two years for seeds to germinate and up to 10 years before a plant is large and strong enough to bloom.

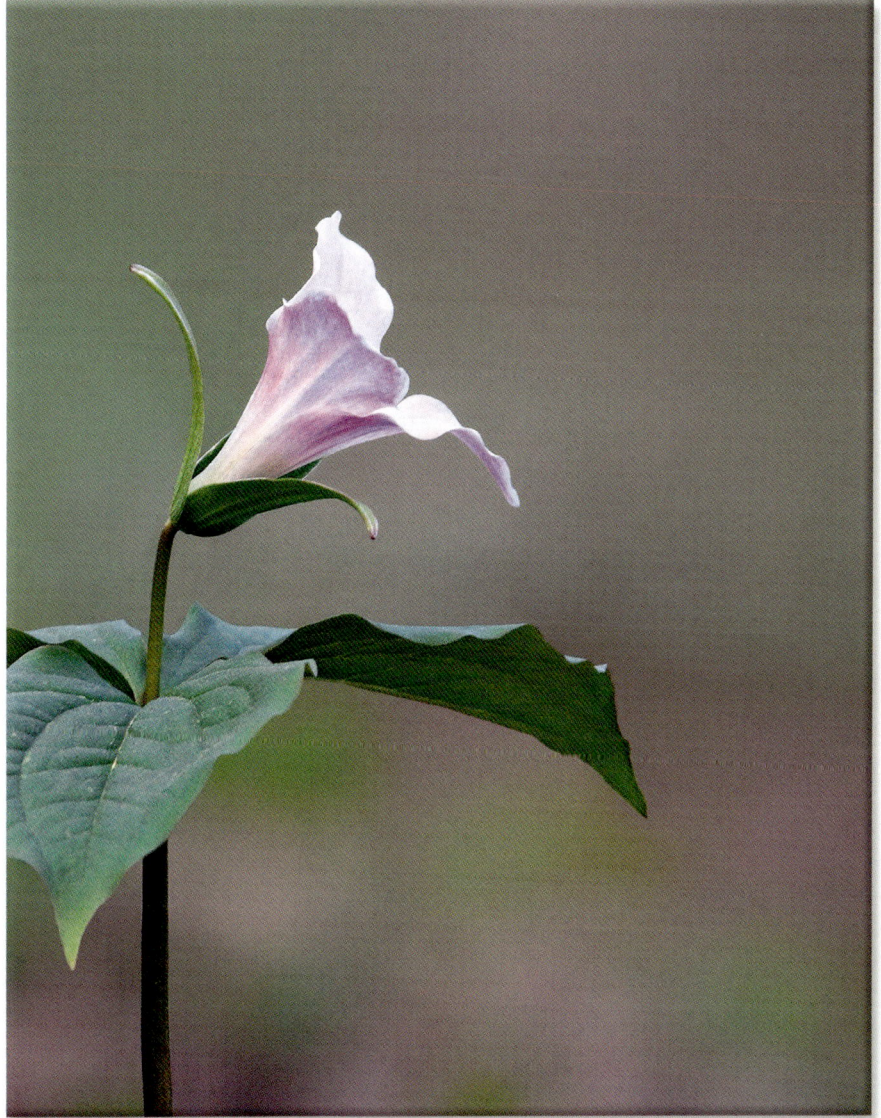

Large-flowered Trillium   *Trillium grandiflorum*

Large-flowered Trillium

Trillium grandiflorum. Large-flowered Trillium offers an example of the importance of symbiotic balance in nature. This handsome member of the Lily family both relies on — and is threatened by — White-tailed Deer. Large-flowered Trillium depends on several creatures to survive. Bumblebees pollinate its flowers and later in the season, black berries appear, bearing seeds. As with violets and other spring species, ants collect and bury the seeds; they eat the fatty appendages called elaiosomes and discard the seeds in underground tunnels — in effect, planting them. But this process, called mymechochory or "ant farming," spreads the seed only a short distance from the mother plant. Deer, on the other hand, may establish plants a mile from the mother, helping assure a greater range for the species. Deer love trillium, eating flowers, leaves and berries. In the process the seeds pass through the digestive system and are deposited, with fertilizer, often far from their source. If deer populations are "normal," only the higher parts of the trillium tend to get eaten. However, in many parts of the eastern United States, the deer herd is so large that Large-flowered Trillium is being eaten to the ground, denying the rootstock the nutrition it needs and killing off colonies.

Large-flowered Trillium   *Trillium grandiflorum*

Wild Columbine

Aquilegia canadensis. "Our columbine is at all times and in all places one of the most exquisitely beautiful of flowers," wrote naturalist John Burroughs more than a century ago. A popular native bird would agree. Many spring wildflowers have developed close relationships with insects, be they bees, butterflies, flies, or even ants. However, in its evolution, the Wild Columbine (*Aquilegia canadensis*) has mostly shunned insects for survival and, perhaps like no other eastern wildflower, has turned to a bird to pollinate its blossoms. Its color and unusual shape are exquisitely designed to attract and serve the Ruby-throated Hummingbird, the only one of 18 North American hummingbird species that nests on the East Coast. Blooming at the same time "hummers" are just arriving from Central and South America, the Wild Columbine displays colors that attract hummingbirds and offers nectar that provides a much-needed energy boost. Red catches the bird's eye, and the yellow opening and interior guide the bird into the flower and to the sweets. Although some bees, wasps, and other insects cheat the system by nibbling through the nectar end of the top spur, only the largest, strongest, and longest-tongued insects, such as bumblebees, can draw sweets from the tube. And, of course, the hummingbird, whose long beak and ability to fly like an insect allow it to hover beneath the blossom and dip up for a sip. These downward facing tubular flowers have another advantage: They do not need to close to protect their nectar and pollen from the rain, which just rolls down their backs. A surprise to many, Wild Columbine is a member of the Buttercup family, whose most common members bear no resemblance.

Wild Columbine   *Aquilegia canadensis*

Virginia Spiderwort

Tradescantia virginiana. Fear not, arachnophobes, Virginia Spiderwort does not attract spiders. Well, no more than any other plant might. However, there's no consensus on just why it's a spiderwort. Some say it's because the long slender leaves, especially when flopped over, look like a squatting spider. Others maintain it's the juice from the leaves – break one and the fluid quickly forms webby threads. Still others believe it's from the weblike filaments surrounding the anthers on the flowers. Less obscure is its scientific name, *Tradescantia virginiana*, which recalls one of the great English botanists and students of newly discovered North American plants. John Tradescant (1608-1662) served as gardener to King Charles I of England; he received and propagated many of the samples of plants from the Colonies. In fact, his son, bearing the same name, traveled to America and collected specimens — and succeeded his father as royal gardener. Over the centuries, hybrids of Virginia Spiderwort and other *Tradescantia* species have been created as garden flowers and even houseplants. Our wild native needs no hybridization to radiate beauty — its three-petaled blossoms may be blue, violet, rose, purple, or rarely even white. This display is a backdrop for six bright yellow stamens, producing a colorful array that attracts a wide variety of bees, many of which provide pollination services. For the American Indians and early settlers, the plant's greens were fried or boiled as food. The roots were mashed to create a poultice to treat skin cancers and even bites by insects — perhaps even by spiders.

Virginia Spiderwort   *Tradescantia virginiana*

Pink Lady's-slipper

Cypripedium acaule. Like many other orchids, the Pink Lady's-slipper or "Moccasin Flower" manipulates insects to pollinate its flowers and produce viable seed. The flower color, vein-like lines and its shape— including the dangling sepals — are all designed to attract bees to enter the labellum or "slipper" through an opening in the top. In the process, past pollen is raked off and new pollen is pasted onto the "captured" bee as it moves through the slipper in one direction — angled hairs discourage its trying to leave the same way it entered. Finally, it reaches and squeezes through a small opening in the rear. For the bee, it's an exhausting operation and discourages visiting a second lady's-slipper. In fact, a University of Maryland botanist, who studied about 3,000 Pink Lady's-slippers in a national forest, found that, over 16 years, about 1,000 of the plants flowered. Of those, a mere 23 were successfully pollinated! How can a species survive with so few seed-producing flowers? Since the average life span of these plants is 20 years, and some may live for a century and a half, lady's-slippers have a long time to turn out one successful flower. And once pollinated, that flower could generate up to 60,000 seeds!

Pink Lady's-slipper   *Cypripedium acaule*

Yellow Lady's-slipper

Cypripedium parviflorum. The Yellow Lady's-slipper has a hard time getting started in life and, once established, has a hard time staying alive. While this orchid is found in most of North America, it is particularly fussy about exactly where it lives, favoring woods that tend to be moist and loamy. The flowers are not often fertilized, and when they are, the resulting seed must have the right "friends" in the soil to sprout. A *Cypripedium* seed is tiny and, unlike most seeds we are familiar with, contains no food. The seed needs to connect with the subterranean threads of a *Rhizoctonia* fungus. If things balance out just right, the fungus digests the outside of the orchid seed, but leaves inner cells untouched. The orchid seed joins with the fungus and starts absorbing nutrients the fungus obtained from the soil. Not until this happens can the seed germinate and begin growing. The symbiosis doesn't end there. For the infant corm to obtain minerals and other soil foods, it must continue to use the "go-between" services of the *Rhizoctonia* fungus. The fungus, in turn, takes from the seedling foods that the young Lady's Slipper leaves have photosynthetically manufactured. Such sensitive and complex relationships make native orchids of all kinds relatively uncommon, and growing them from seed requires a real expert. What's more, in the wild it can take 10 or more years for a Lady's-slipper orchid to be strong enough to bloom. If those aren't tough enough survival odds, there are the deer. In a few seconds, a White-tailed Deer can gobble down a Lady's-slipper that took years to grow. This has become a major problem in the East where burgeoning deer populations have been devastating many native wildflowers — especially Yellow and Pink Lady's-slippers.

Yellow Lady's-slipper *Cypripedium parviflorum*

Virginia Waterleaf

Hydrophyllum virginianum. Unlike birds, which have an international agency to establish appropriate common names for each species, plants just go with the flow. Such is the case with Virginia Waterleaf (*Hydrophyllum virginianum*), which is also known as Eastern Waterleaf, Shawnee Salad, John's Cabbage, and a half dozen other folk names. Worse, perhaps, is the fact that no one can seem to settle on the reason for "waterleaf" (which is also the meaning of *Hydrophyllum*). One explanation is that its large lower leaves are designed to gather in the drip from the trees overhead, keeping the roots well watered. Another is that the type species for this genus has watery leaves. Still another is that the white spots on the leaves look like water stains! Those leaves unfold early in the spring, but it's not till late spring that the clusters of eight to 20 bell-shaped flowers of white, pink or light purple appear. Various techniques, such as the shape of the flower and positioning of the stamens, are designed to attract and use bees for pollination, while other techniques, such as hairiness of the flowers, discourage smaller nectar-hungry insects. In fact, the waterleaf has an insect virtually all of its own — the Waterleaf Cuckoo Bee. This bee relies on the waterleaf so much that it's been given the name *Nomada hydrophylli*. And, no, it's not cuckoo over waterleaves. Its common name comes from the fact that it practices cleptoparasitism. Like the cuckoo bird that lays its eggs in the nests of other species that wind up raising the cuckoo chicks, the Nomada lay their eggs on the pollen stores in the nests of other bee species. Thus, in effect, the other bees wind up feeding and raising the Nomada babies.

Virginia Waterleaf   *Hydrophyllum virginianum*

Yellow Stargrass

Hypoxis hirsuta. In mid-spring, as the leaves begin appearing on the deciduous forest trees, the Yellow Stargrass brings bursts of yellow to the forest floor. A small but brilliant perennial, Yellow Stargrass bears grass-like leaves that are similar to those of the Blue-eyed Grass. However, though it has also been placed in the Lily family as well as the Amaryllis clan, the genus *Hypoxis* is sometimes classified in a family of its own.

Hypoxis hirsuta seems to have found little use among man or beast; it is not known to have been employed as a herbal medicine and wildlife seem to shun its leaves, perhaps in part because of their hairs — hence *"hirsuta"* or "hairy" — or maybe because of their flavor. Visible clearly in this picture, the hairs on the stems and on the flowers' six yellow tepals (sepals that look like petals) may also have evolved for another purpose: To entangle the feet of crawling insects like ants, thus dissuading them from pilfering pollen. The nectarless blossom uses pollen to attract its only fans — flying insects such as small bees, flies and beetles that can provide the pollination services that crawlers can't. Yellow Stargrass is found in most states east of the Rockies.

Yellow Stargrass   *Hypoxis hirsuta*

Blue-eyed Grass

Sisyrinchium angustifolium. Blue-eyed Grass is a pleasant name for a pretty flower that, because of its small size, is often overlooked in the spring landscape. Many species of the genus *Sisyrinchium* live in North America. Among them, *Sisyrinchium angustifolium*, called Slender, Narrow-leaf or Stout Blue-eyed Grass, shown here, may be the most common and widespread, found in every state east of the Mississippi River and some to the west. Although commonly found in meadows and fields, *S. angusifolium* also does well in damp woods, where its six blue-violet petals tend to be deeper in color than the hue found in sunnier sites. (Some members of the Blue-eyed Grass genus aren't blue at all, but yellow or white, leading to names like Golden-eyed Grass or the strange moniker, White Blue-eyed Grass, a flower that has no blue at all!) Plants are sometimes found in small clusters, but often in colonies bearing hundreds of blossoms, making up in numbers what they lack in size. The long, slender leaves look like grass, but are actually tiny versions of the leaves typically found on fellow members of the Iris family. Among the American Indians, this plant treated stomach and digestive problems, including diarrhea and worms. According to 17th Century herbalist John Gerard, Europeans used masses of the tiny bulbs of a close cousin, *S. majus*, now often called *Moraea sisyrinchium*, for a less practical purpose: An aphrodisiac "to procure lust and lecherie."

Blue-eyed Grass   *Sisyrinchium angustifolium*

Whorled Loosestrife

Lysimachia quadrifolia. Some wildflowers are known for their color, their size, shape, or scent. Whorled Loosestrife, however, might be best known for its display: It's both elegant and symmetrical. The five-petaled blossoms are star-shaped and yellow, streaked with red especially near the centers — guides for approaching insects. Each flower projects from the stalk on a long, thin but strong stem, from above each of four leaves, with each leaf usually growing exactly 90 degrees from two others. These layers of whorled leaves and flowers appear all along the two- to three-foot tall stalk, gaining the plant its other common name of Crosswort, and contributing to the botanic name, *Lysimachia quadrifolia*. *Lysimachia* is Greek for "loose-strife." Some authorities believe the plant was named for King Lysimachus of Sicily because he used it for healing wounds gained in fighting — or strife. Another theory says the king employed the herb to calm unruly animals, especially bulls. Seventeenth Century English herbalist John Parkinson wrote, "it is believed to take away strife or debate between ye beasts, not only those that are yoked together, but even those that are wild also, by making them tame and quiet." Margaret Grieve, a more modern herbalist, added, "the plant appears to be obnoxious to gnats and flies, and so, no doubt, placing it under yoke, relieved the beasts of their tormentors, thus making them quiet and tractable." She recommended dried loosestrife be burnt in houses to get rid of gnats and flies. The perennial blooms in thickets and at the edges of woods during June and July throughout most of eastern North America.

Whorled Loosestrife

Lysimachia quadrifolia

Canada Lily

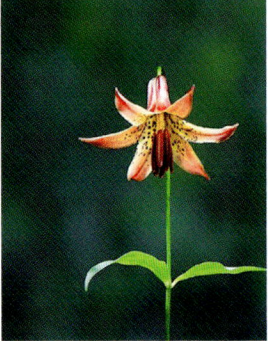

Lilium canadense. Many flowers contain subtle design techniques to help insure their survival. However, little is subtle about the Canada Lily, both in the ways it attracts pollinators and the method it uses to protect what those visitors want. The bell-shaped flowers, up to 16 of them blooming on a single plant, are bright yellow, orange or red. Both color and a sweet scent attract a variety of insects, but especially butterflies like the Great Spangled Fritillary, which love its nectar and transfer its sticky pollen during visits. The shape and color - especially redder versions like the one here - also attract Ruby-throated Hummingbirds. To keep the nectar and pollen safe, the Canada Lily also evolved its downward-facing flower, with a tightly sealed and shiny surface at the top of the "bell." Rain rolls off the blossom like an umbrella. A native of eastern North America - not just Canada, where it was probably first identified - *Lilium canadense* blooms in mid-summer, favoring partial sunlight of wetlands, including meadows and fields. Once common, it is becoming harder to find in many parts of its range because of overpopulating deer, which often eat the young shoots after they emerge from the ground. In Canada, it is on an endangered species list. American Indians employed the plant both as a medicine and food, using the root for a tea that treated stomach ailments, rheumatism and other problems, and grinding the bulbs to create flour that would thicken soups.

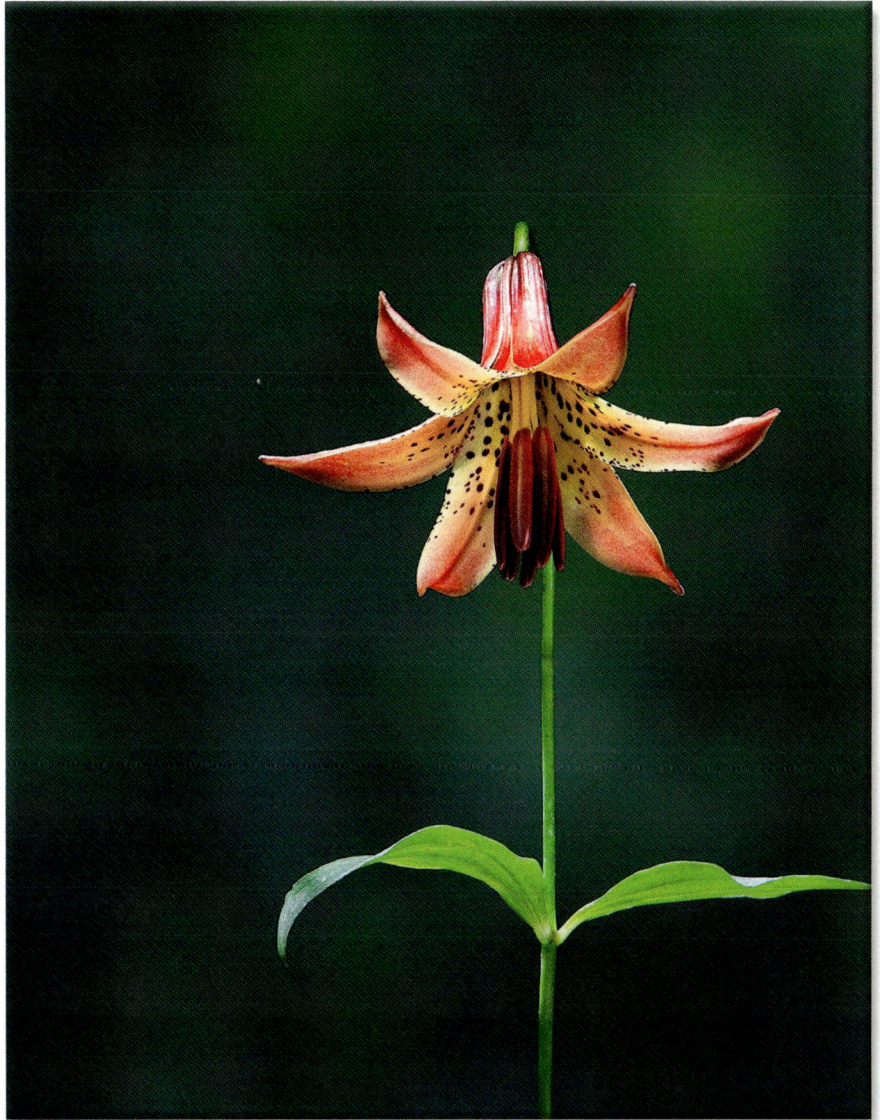

Canada Lily   *Lilium canadense*

Turk's-cap Lily

Lilium superbum. You may have a hard time finding a Turk wearing a hat that looks like the Turk's-cap Lily, but if you happen by a produce stand in the early autumn, look for Turk's Cap squash - it bears a remarkeable resemblance to this late-spring wildflower. The common name is colorful, but the botanical name is more apt and easily understood: *Lilium superbum*. It means a lily that's "noble," "excellent," "proud," or even "lofty." All descriptions apply to this giant among native lilies - it can reach 10 feet in height and bear as many as 40 large, dangling flowers that may range from yellow through orange to red. Though somewhat different in design to the related Canada Lily, the Turk's-cap attracts many of the same pollinators: Ruby-throated Hummingbirds, large butterflies, and moths - especially the hawk moths known as Hummingbird Moths. And like other large lilies, its starchy bulbs have been used in making soup. Turk's-cap Lily seems most common in the Mid-Atlantic states, though it can be found out to and just beyond the middle Mississippi River region and into Florida. And as winters get warmer, it may spread into northern New England - if it can survive the deer, which love not the beauty but the flavor of this flower. Often confused with the common Tiger Lily, an imported garden escape, it is sometimes called the American Tiger Lily.

Turk's-cap Lily   *Lilium superbum*

Spotted Jewelweed

Impatiens capensis. Some say spotted jewelweed is so called because the colorful orange flowers dangle from the plant like earrings or pendants. Others maintain it's because the edges of the leaves, when wet with dew or rain, hold the tiny drops of water that look like "scintillating gems, dancing, sparkling in the sunshine," as one naturalist put it over a century ago. But it is also called Touch-Me-Not and no wonder: The seeds are housed in an ingenious case that, when mature and disturbed, suddenly "pops" like an uncoiling spring. The action sends the seeds flying as far as four or five feet, which is why spotted jewelweed can easily become widespread. Spotted jewelweed is famous as a balm to relieve the itching caused by poison ivy. Colonial Americans used the juice to dye wool yellow, and ate the leaves as a potherb. In nature, its biggest admirer is the Ruby-throated Hummingbird, which thrives on its flowers in late spring and summer. Evolution has designed those flowers to be pollinated by the bill of the hummingbird, which picks up the grains of white pollen from just inside the top front of one flower and deposits them on the inside top of the next. Its official name is *Impatiens capensis*, which oddly enough means "of the Cape of Good Hope." The plant namer mistakenly thought his samples came from South Africa instead of North America. In the interests of stability, the International Code of Botanical Nomenclature does not permit changes in the specific name merely because it's 'inappropriate.' Thus, we have a North American plant with a South African name.

Spotted Jewelweed   *Impatiens capensis*

"I only went out for a walk, and finally concluded to stay out till sundown, for going out, I found, was really going in."

-- John Muir

Plant Notes

Bloodroot
Sanguinaria canadensis

Poppy Family
(Papaveraceae)

6-12 inches
March-May

Round-lobed Hepatica
Hepatica americana

Buttercup Family
(Ranunculaceae)

4-6 inches
March-May

Trout Lily
Erythronium americanum

Lily Family
(Liliaceae)

4-10 inches
March-May

Dwarf Iris
Iris verna

Iris Family
(Iridaceae)

2-6 inches
March-May

Spring Beauty
Claytonia virginica

Purslane Family
(Portulacaceae)

6-12 inches
March - May

Common Blue Violet
Viola sororia

Violet Family
(Violaceae)

3-8 inches
March-June

Rue-anemone
Thalictrum thalictroides

Buttercup Family
(Ranunculaceae)

4-8 inches
March-May

Twinleaf
Jeffersonia diphylla

Barberry Family
(Berberidaceae)

8 inches
April-May

Virginia Bluebell
Mertensia virginica

Forget-Me-Not Family
(Boraginaceae)

12-24 inches
March-May

Dutchman's Breeches
Dicentra cucullaria

Poppy Family
(Papaveraceae)

5-9 inches
April-May

Yellow Fumewort
Corydalis flavula

Poppy Family
(Papaveraceae)

6-16 inches
April-May

Mayapple
Podophyllum peltatum

Barberry Family
(Berberidaceae)

12-18 inches
April-June

Wild Geranium
Geranium maculatum

Geranium Family
(Geraniaceae)

12-24 inches
April-June

Cut-leaf Toothwort
Cardamine concetenata

Mustard Family
(Cruciferae)

8-15 inches
April-June

Showy Orchis
Orchis spectabilis

Orchid Family
(Orchidaceae)

4-12 inches
April-June

Downy Yellow Violet
Viola pubescens

Violet Family
(Violaceae)

12-18 inches
April-June

Bird's-foot Violet
Viola pedata

Violet Family
(Violaceae)

4-10 inches
April-June

Large-flowered Trillium
Trillium grandiflorum

Lily Family
(Liliaceae)

12-18 inches
April-June

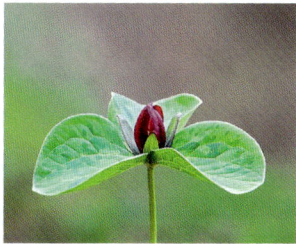

Little Sweet Betsy
Trillium cuneatum

Lily Family
(Liliaceae)

4-12 inches
April-June

Wild Columbine
Aquilegia canadensis

Buttercup Family
(Ranunculaceae)

1-2 feet
April-July

Large-flowered Trillium
Trillium grandiflorum

Lily Family
(Liliaceae)

12-18 inches
April-June

Virginia Spiderwort
Tradescantia virginiana

Spiderwort Family
(Commelinaceae)

8-24 inches
April-July

Pink Lady's-slipper
Cypripedium acaule

Orchid Family
(Orchidaceae)

6-15 inches
May-June

Yellow Stargrass
Hypoxis hirsuta

Lily Family
(Liliaceae)

1-12 inches
May-August

Yellow Lady's-slipper
Cypripedium parviflorum

Orchid Family
(Orchidaceae)

18-24 inches
May-July

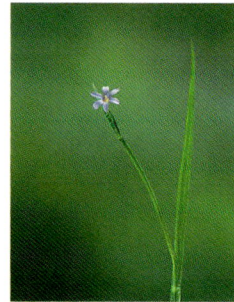

Blue-eyed Grass
Sisyrinchium angustifolium

Iris Family
(Iridaceae)

18-24 inches
June-July

Virginia Waterleaf
Hydrophyllum virginianum

Waterleaf Family
(Hydrophyllaceae)

1-3 feet
May-August

Whorled Loosestrife
Lysimachia quadrifolia

Primrose Family
(Primulaceae)

1-3 feet
June-August

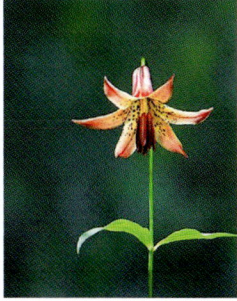

Canada Lily
Lilium canadense

Lily Family
(Liliaceae)

2-5 feet
June-August

Spotted Jewelweed
Impatiens capensis

Touch-Me-Not Family
(Balsaminaceae)

2-5 feet
July-September

Turk's-cap Lily
Lilium superbum

Lily Family
(Liliaceae)

3-8 feet
July-August

Plant State Index

Alabama (30)
Bloodroot, Trout Lily, Round-lobed Hepatica, Dwarf Iris, Spring Beauty, Rue-anemone, Virginia Bluebell, Common Blue Violet, Twinleaf, Dutchman's Breeches, Yellow Fumewort, Wild Geranium, Showy Orchis, Mayapple, Cut-leaf Toothwort, Downy Yellow Violet, Bird's-foot Violet, Little Sweet Betsy, Large-flowered Trillium, Wild Columbine, Virginia Spiderwort, Pink Lady's-slipper, Yellow Lady's-slipper, Virginia Waterleaf, Yellow Stargrass, Blue-eyed Grass, Whorled Loosestrife, Canada Lily, Turk's-cap Lily, Spotted Jewelweed

Alaska (1)
Yellow Lady's-slipper

Arizona (1)
Yellow Lady's-slipper

Arkansas (26)
Bloodroot, Trout Lily, Round-lobed Hepatica, Dwarf Iris, Spring Beauty, Rue-anemone, Virginia Bluebell, Common Blue Violet, Dutchman's Breeches, Yellow Fumewort, Wild Geranium, Showy Orchis, Mayapple, Cut-leaf Toothwort, Downy Yellow Violet, Bird's-foot Violet, Little Sweet Betsy, Wild Columbine, Virginia Spiderwort, Yellow Lady's-slipper, Virginia Waterleaf, Yellow Stargrass, Blue-eyed Grass, Canada Lily, Turk's-cap Lily, Spotted Jewelweed

California (1)
Virginia Spiderwort

Colorado (3)
Yellow Lady's-slipper, Yellow Stargrass, Spotted Jewelweed

Connecticut (26)
Bloodroot, Trout Lily, Round-lobed Hepatica, Spring Beauty, Rue-anemone, Common Blue Violet, Dutchman's Breeches, Yellow Fumewort, Wild Geranium, Showy Orchis, Mayapple, Cut-leaf Toorthwort, Downy Yellow Violet, Bird's-foot Violet, Large-flowered Trillium, Wild Columbine, Virginia Spiderwort, Pink Lady's-slipper, Yellow Lady's-slipper, Virginia Waterleaf, Yellow Stargrass, Blue-eyed Grass, Whorled Loosestrife, Canada Lily, Turk's-cap Lily, Spotted Jewelweed

Delaware (27)
Bloodroot, Trout Lily, Round-lobed Hepatica, Spring Beauty, Rue-anemone, Virginia Bluebell, Common Blue Violet, Dutchman's Breeches, Yellow Fumewort, Wild Geranium, Showy Orchis, Mayapple, Cut-leaf Toothwort, Downy Yellow Violet, Bird's-foot Violet, Large-flowered Trillium, Wild Columbine, Virginia Spiderwort, Pink Lady's-slipper, Yellow Lady's-slipper, Virginia Waterleaf, Yellow Stargrass, Blue-eyed Grass, Whorled Loosestrife, Canada Lily, Turk's-cap Lily, Spotted Jewelweed

District of Columbia (30)
Bloodroot, Trout Lily, Round-lobed Hepatica, Dwarf Iris, Spring Beauty, Rue-anemone, Virginia Bluebell, Common Blue Violet, Twinleaf, Dutchman's Breeches, Yellow Fumewort, Wild Geranium, Showy Orchis, Mayapple, Cut-leaf Toothwort, Downy Yellow Violet, Bird's-foot Violet, Little Sweet Betsy, Large-flowered Trillium, Wild Columbine, Virginia Spiderwort, Pink Lady's-slipper, Yellow Lady's-slipper, Virginia Waterleaf, Yellow Stargrass, Blue-eyed Grass, Whorled Loosestrife, Canada Lily, Turk's-cap Lily, Spotted Jewelweed

Florida (12)
Bloodroot, Round-lobed Hepatica, Dwarf Iris, Rue-anemone, Common Blue Violet, Yellow Fomewort, Mayapple, Cut-leaf Toothwort, Wild Columbine, Blue-eyed Grass, Turk's-cap Lily, Spotted Jewelweed

Georgia (27)
Bloodroot, Round-lobed Hepatica, Dwarf Iris, Spring Beauty, Rue-anemone, Virginia Bluebell, Common Blue Violet, Twinleaf, Dutchman's Breeches, Yellow Fumewort, Wild Geranium, Showy Orchis, Mayapple, Cut-leaf Toothwort, Downy Yellow Violet, Bird's-foot Violet, Large-flowered Trillium, Wild Columbine, Virginia Spiderwort, Pink Lady's-slipper, Yellow Lady's slipper, Yellow Stargrass, Blue-eyed Grass, Whorled Loosestrife, Canada Lily, Turk's-cap Lily, Spotted Jewelweed

Hawaii (0)

Idaho (3)
Dutchman's Breeches, Yellow Lady's-slipper, Spotted Jewelweed

Iowa (23)
Bloodroot, Trout Lily, Round-lobed Hepatica, Spring Beauty, Rue-anemone, Virginia Bluebell, Common Blue Violet, Twinleaf, Dutchman's Breeches, Yellow Fumewort, Wild Geranium, Showy Orchis, Mayapple, Cut-leaf Toothwort, Downy Yellow Violet, Bird's-foot Violet, Wild Columbine, Virginia Spiderwort, Yellow Lady's-slipper, Virginia Waterleaf, Yellow Stargrass, Blue-eyed Grass, Spotted Jewelweed

Illinois (28)
Bloodroot, Trout Lily, Round-lobed Hepatica, Spring Beauty, Rue-anemone, Virginia Bluebell, Common Blue Violet, Twinleaf, Dutchman's Breeches, Yellow Fumewort, Wild Geranium, Showy Orchis, Mayapple, Cut-leaf Toothwort, Downy Yellow Violet, Bird's-foot Violet, Little Sweet Betsy, Large-flowered Trillium, Wild Columbine, Virginia Spiderwort, Pink Lady's-slipper, Yellow Lady's-slipper, Virginia Waterleaf, Yellow Stargrass, Blue-eyed Grass, Whorled Loosestrife, Turk's-cap Lily, Spotted Jewelweed

Kansas (21)
Bloodroot, Spring Beauty, Rue-anemone, Virginia Bluebell, Common Blue Violet, Dutchman's Breeches, Yellow Fumewort, Wild Geranium, Showy Orchis, Mayapple, Cut-leaf Toothwort, Downy Yellow Violet, Bird's-foot Violet, Little Sweet Betsy, Wild Columbine, Yellow Lady's-slipper, Virginia Waterleaf, Yellow Stargrass, Blue-eyed Grass, Canada Lily, Spotted Jewelweed

Indiana (29)
Bloodroot, Trout Lily, Round-lobed Hepatica, Spring Beauty, Rue-anemone, Virginia Bluebell, Common Blue Violet, Twinleaf, Dutchman's Breeches, Yellow Fumewort, Wild Geranium, Showy Orchis, Mayapple, Cut-leaf Toothwort, Downy Yellow Violet, Bird's-foot Violet, Little Sweet Betsy, Large-flowered Trillium, Wild Columbine, Virginia Spiderwort, Pink Lady's-slipper, Yellow Lady's-slipper, Virginia Waterleaf, Yellow Stargrass, Blue-eyed Grass, Whorled Loosestrife, Canada Lily, Turk's-cap Lily, Spotted Jewelweed

Kentucky (30)
Bloodroot, Trout Lily, Round-lobed Hepatica, Dwarf Iris, Spring Beauty, Rue-anemone, Virginia Bluebell, Common Blue Violet, Twinleaf, Dutchman's Breeches, Yellow Fumewort, Wild Geranium, Showy Orchis, Mayapple, Cut-leaf Toothwort, Downy Yellow Violet, Bird's-foot Violet, Little Sweet Betsy, Large-flowered Trillium, Wild Columbine, Virginia Spiderwort, Pink Lady's-slipper, Yellow Lady's-slipper, Virginia Waterleaf, Yellow Stargrass, Blue-eyed Grass, Whorled Loosestrife, Canada Lily, Turk's-cap Lily, Spotted Jewelweed

Louisiana (13)

Bloodroot, Spring Beauty, Common Blue Violet, Yellow Fumewort, Wild Geranium, Mayapple, Cut-leaf Toothwort, Downy Yellow Violet, Bird's-foot Violet, Virginia Spiderwort, Yellow Stargrass, Blue-eyed Grass, Spotted Jewelweed

Maine (23)

Bloodroot, Trout Lily, Round-lobed Hepatica, Rue-anemone, Virginia Bluebell, Common Blue Violet, Dutchman's Breeches, Wild Geranium, Showy Orchis, Mayapple, Cut-leaf Toothwort, Downy Yellow Violet, Bird's-foot Violet, Large-flowered Trillium, Wild Columbine, Virginia Spiderwort, Pink Lady's-slipper, Yellow Lady's-slipper, Yellow Stargrass, Blue-eyed Grass, Whorled Loosestrife, Canada Lily, Spotted Jewelweed

Maryland (30)

Bloodroot, Trout Lily, Round-lobed Hepatica, Dwarf Iris, Spring Beauty, Rue-anemone, Virginia Bluebell, Common Blue Violet, Twinleaf, Dutchman's Breeches, Yellow Fumewort, Wild Geranium, Showy Orchis, Mayapple, Cut-leaf Toothwort, Downy Yellow Violet, Bird's-foot Violet, Little Sweet Betsy, Large-flowered Trillium, Wild Columbine, Virginia Spiderwort, Pink Lady's-slipper, Yellow Lady's-slipper, Virginia Waterleaf, Yellow Stargrass, Blue-eyed Grass, Whorled Loosestrife, Canada Lily, Turk's-cap Lily, Spotted Jewelweed

Massachusetts (26)

Bloodroot, Trout Lily, Round-lobed Hepatica, Spring Beauty, Rue-anemone, Virginia Bluebell, Common Blue Violet, Dutchman's Breeches, Wild Geranium, Showy Orchis, Mayapple, Cut-leaf Toothwort, Downy Yellow Violet, Bird's-foot Violet, Large-flowered Trillium, Wild Columbine, Virginia Spiderwort, Pink Lady's-slipper, Yellow Lady's-slipper, Virginia Waterleaf, Yellow Stargrass, Blue-eyed Grass, Whorled Loosestrife, Canada Lily, Turk's-cap Lily, Spotted Jewelweed

Michigan (27)

Bloodroot, Trout Lily, Round-lobed Hepatica, Spring Beauty, Rue-anemone, Virginia Bluebell, Common Blue Violet, Twinleaf, Dutchman's Breeches, Yellow Fumewort, Wild Geranium, Showy Orchis, Mayapple, Cut-leaf Toothwort, Downy Yellow Violet, Bird's-foot Violet, Little Sweet Betsy, Large-flowered Trillium, Wild Columbine, Virginia Spiderwort, Pink Lady's slipper, Yellow Lady's-slipper, Virginia Waterleaf, Yellow Stargrass, Blue-eyed Grass, Whorled Loosestrife, Spotted Jewelweed

Minnesota (25)

Bloodroot, Trout Lily, Round-lobed Hepatica, Spring Beauty, Rue-anemone, Virginia Bluebell, Common Blue Violet, Twinleaf, Dutchman's Breeches, Wild Geranium, Showy Orchis, Mayapple, Cut-leaf Toothwort, Downy Yellow Violet, Bird's-foot Violet, Large-flowered Trillium, Wild Columbine, Virginia Spiderwort, Pink Lady's-slipper, Yellow Lady's-slipper, Virginia Waterleaf, Yellow Stargrass, Blue-eyed Grass, Whorled Loosestrife, Spotted Jewelweed

Mississippi (22)

Bloodroot, Round-lobed Hepatica, Dwarf Iris, Spring Beauty, Rue-anemone, Virginia Bluebell, Common Blue Violet, Dutchman's Breeches, Yellow Fumewort, Wild Geranium, Showy Orchis, Mayapple, Cut-leaf Toothwort, Downy Yellow Violet, Bird's-foot Violet, Wild Columbine, Virginia Spiderwort, Yellow Lady's-slipper, Yellow Stargrass, Blue-eyed Grass, Turk's-cap Lily, Spotted Jewelweed

Missouri (25)

Bloodroot, Trout Lily, Round-lobed Hepatica, Dwarf Iris, Spring Beauty, Rue-anemone, Virginia Bluebell, Common Blue Violet, Dutchman's Breeches, Yellow Fumewort, Wild Geranium, Showy Orchis, Mayapple, Cut-leaf Toothwort, Downy Yellow Violet, Bird's-foot Violet, Little Sweet Betsy, Wild Columbine, Virginia Spiderwort, Yellow Lady's-slipper, Virginia Waterleaf, Yellow Stargrass, Blue-eyed Grass, Turk's-cap Lily, Spotted Jewelweed

Montana (1)

Yellow Lady's-slipper

Nebraska (16)

Bloodroot, Spring Beauty, Common Blue Violet, Dutchman's Breeches, Yellow Fumewort, Showy Orchis, Mayapple, Cut-leaf Toothwort, Downy Yellow Violet, Bird's-foot Violet, Wild Columbine, Yellow Lady's-slipper, Virginia Waterleaf, Yellow Stargrass, Canada Lily, Spotted Jewelweed

Nevada (0)

New Hampshire (24)

Bloodroot, Trout Lily, Round-lobed Hepatica, Rue-anemone, Common Blue Violet, Dutchman's Breeches, Wild Geranium, Showy Orchis, Mayapple, Cut-leaf Toothwort, Downy Yellow Violet, Bird's-foot Violet, Large-flowered Trillium, Wild Columbine, Virginia Spiderwort, Pink Lady's-slipper, Yellow Lady's-slipper, Virginia Waterleaf, Yellow Stargrass, Blue-eyed Grass, Whorled Loosestrife, Canada Lily, Turk's-cap Lily, Spotted Jewelweed

New Jersey (27)

Bloodroot, Trout Lily, Round-lobed Hepatica, Spring Beauty, Rue-anemone, Virginia Bluebell, Common Blue Violet, Twinleaf, Dutchman's Breeches, Yellow Fumewort, Showy Orchis, Mayapple, Cut-leaf Toothwort, Downy Yellow Violet, Bird's-foot Violet, Large-flowered Trillium, Wild Columbine, Virginia Spiderwort, Pink Lady's-slipper, Yellow Lady's-slipper, Virginia Waterleaf, Yellow Stargrass, Blue-eyed Grass, Whorled Loosestrife, Canada Lily, Turk's-cap Lily, Spotted Jewelweed

New Mexico (2)

Yellow Lady's-slipper, Yellow Stargrass

New York (30)

Bloodroot, Trout Lily, Round-lobed Hepatica, Dwarf Iris, Spring Beauty, Rue-anemone, Virginia Bluebell, Common Blue Violet, Twinleaf, Dutchman's Breeches, Yellow Fumewort, Wild Geranium, Showy Orchis, Mayapple, Cut-leaf Toothwort, Downy Yellow Violet, Bird's-foot Violet, Little Sweet Betsy, Large-flowered Trillium, Wild Columbine, Virginia Spiderwort, Pink Lady's-slipper, Yellow Lady's-slipper, Virginia Waterleaf, Yellow Stargrass, Blue-eyed Grass, Whorled Loosestrife, Canada Lily, Turk's-cap Lily, Spotted Jewelweed

North Carolina (30)

Bloodroot, Trout Lily, Round-lobed Hepatica, Dwarf Iris, Spring Beauty, Rue-anemone, Virginia Bluebell, Common Blue Violet, Twinleaf, Dutchman's Breeches, Yellow Fumewort, Wild Geranium, Showy Orchis, Mayapple, Cut-leaf Toothwort, Downy Yellow Violet, Bird's-foot Violet, Little Sweet Betsy, Large-flowered Trillium, Wild Columbine, Virginia Spiderwort, Pink Lady's-slipper, Yellow Lady's-slipper, Virginia Waterleaf, Yellow Stargrass, Blue-eyed Grass, Whorled Loosestrife, Canada Lily, Turk's-cap Lily, Spotted Jewelweed

North Dakota (11)

Bloodroot, Common Blue Violet, Dutchman's Breeches, Wild Geranium, Cut-leaf Toothwort, Downy Yellow Violet, Wild Columbine, Yellow Lady's-slipper, Virginia Waterleaf, Yellow Stargrass, Spotted Jewelweed

Ohio (30)

Bloodroot, Trout Lily, Round-lobed Hepatica, Dwarf Iris, Spring Beauty, Rue-anemone, Virginia Bluebell, Common Blue Violet, Twinleaf, Dutchman's Breeches, Yellow Fumewort, Wild Geranium, Showy Orchis, Mayapple, Cut-leaf Toothwort, Downy Yellow Violet, Bird's-foot Violet, Little Sweet Betsy, Large-flowered Trillium, Wild Columbine, Virginia Spiderwort, Pink Lady's-slipper, Yellow Lady's-slipper, Virginia Waterleaf, Yellow Stargrass, Blue-eyed Grass, Whorled Loosestrife, Canada Lily, Turk's-cap Lily, Spotted Jewelweed

Oklahoma (18)

Bloodroot, Spring Beauty, Rue-anemone, Common Blue Violet, Dutchman's Breeches, Yellow Fumewort, Wild Geranium, Showy Orchis, Mayapple, Cut-leaf Toothwort, Downy Yellow Violet, Bird's-foot Violet, Little Sweet Betsy, Wild Columbine, Virginia Waterleaf, Yellow Stargrass, Blue-eyed Grass, Spotted Jewelweed

Oregon (3)

Dutchman's Breeches, Wild Geranium, Spotted Jewelweed

Pennsylvania (30)

Bloodroot, Trout Lily, Round-lobed Hepatica, Dwarf Iris, Spring Beauty, Rue-anemone, Virginia Bluebell, Common Blue Violet, Twinleaf, Dutchman's Breeches, Yellow Fumewort, Wild Geranium, Showy Orchis, Mayapple, Cut-leaf Toothwort, Downy Yellow Violet, Bird's-foot Violet, Little Sweet Betsy, Large-flowered Trillium, Wild Columbine, Virginia Spiderwort, Pink Lady's-slipper, Yellow Lady's-slipper, Virginia Waterleaf, Yellow Stargrass, Blue-eyed Grass, Whorled Loosestrife, Canada Lily, Turk's-cap Lily, Spotted Jewelweed

Rhode Island (23)

Bloodroot, Trout Lily, Round-lobed Hepatica, Spring Beauty, Rue-anemone, Virginia Bluebell, Common Blue Violet, Dutchman's Breeches, Wild Geranium, Showy Orchis, Mayapple, Downy Yellow Violet, Bird's-foot Violet, Wild Columbine, Virginia Spiderwort, Pink Lady's-slipper, Yellow Lady's-slipper, Yellow Stargrass, Blue-eyed Grass, Whorled Loosestrife, Canada Lily, Turk's-cap Lily, Spotted Jewelweed

South Carolina (26)

Bloodroot, Trout Lily, Round-lobed Hepatica, Dwarf Iris, Spring Beauty, Rue-anemone, Virginia Bluebell, Common Blue Violet, Dutchman's Breeches, Yellow Fumewort, Wild Geranium, Showy Orchis, Mayapple, Cut-leaf Toothwort, Downy Yellow Violet, Bird's-foot Violet, Large-flowered Trillium, Wild Columbine, Virginia Spiderwort, Pink Lady's-slipper, Yellow Lady's-slipper, Yellow Stargrass, Blue-eyed Grass, Whorled Loosestrife, Canada Lily, Spotted Jewelweed

South Dakota (11)

Bloodroot, Virginia Bluebell, Common Blue Violet, Dutchman's Breeches, Cut-leaf Toothwort, Downy Yellow Violet, Wild Columbine, Yellow Lady's-slipper, Virginia Waterleaf, Yellow Stargrass, Spotted Jewelweed

Tennessee (30)

Bloodroot, Trout Lily, Round-lobed Hepatica, Dwarf Iris, Spring Beauty, Rue-anemone, Virginia Bluebell, Common Blue Violet, Twinleaf, Dutchman's Breeches, Yellow Fumewort, Wild Geranium, Showy Orchis, Mayapple, Cut-leaf Toothwort, Downy Yellow Violet, Bird's-foot Violet, Little Sweet Betsy, Large-flowered Trillium, Wild Columbine, Virginia Spiderwort, Pink Lady's-slipper, Yellow Lady's-slipper, Virginia Waterleaf, Yellow Stargrass, Blue-eyed Grass, Whorled Loosestrife, Canada Lily, Turk's-cap Lily, Spotted Jewelweed

Texas (13)

Bloodroot, Spring Beauty, Rue-anemone, Common Blue Violet, Mayapple, Cut-leaf Toothwort, Downy Yellow Violet, Bird's-foot Violet, Wild Columbine, Yellow Lady's-slipper, Yellow Stargrass, Blue-eyed Grass, Spotted Jewelweed

Utah (1)

Yellow Lady's-slipper

Vermont (24)

Bloodroot, Trout Lily, Round-lobed Hepatica, Spring Beauty, Rue-anemone, Virginia Bluebell, Common Blue Violet, Dutchman's Breeches, Wild Geranium, Showy Orchis, Mayapple, Cut-leaf Toothwort, Downy Yellow Violet, Large-flowered Trillium, Wild Columbine, Virginia Spiderwort, Pink Lady's-slipper, Yellow Lady's-slipper, Virginia Waterleaf, Yellow Stargrass, Blue-eyed Grass, Whorled Loosestrife, Canada Lily, Spotted Jewelweed

Virginia (30)

Bloodroot, Trout Lily, Round-lobed Hepatica, Dwarf Iris, Spring Beauty, Rue-anemone, Virginia Bluebell, Common Blue Violet, Twinleaf, Dutchman's Breeches, Yellow Fumewort, Wild Geranium, Showy Orchis, Mayapple, Cut-leaf Toothwort, Downy Yellow Violet, Bird's-foot Violet, Little Sweet Betsy, Large-flowered Trillium, Wild Columbine, Virginia Spiderwort, Pink Lady's-slipper, Yellow Lady's-slipper, Virginia Waterleaf, Yellow Stargrass, Blue-eyed Grass, Whorled Loosestrife, Canada Lily, Turk's-cap Lily, Spotted Jewelweed

Washington (4)

Virginia Bluebell, Dutchman's Breeches, Yellow Lady's-slipper, Spotted Jewelweed

West Virginia (30)
Bloodroot, Trout Lily, Round-lobed Hepatica, Dwarf Iris, Spring Beauty, Rue-anemone, Virginia Bluebell, Common Blue Violet, Twinleaf, Dutchman's Breeches, Yellow Fumewort, Wild Geranium, Showy Orchis, Mayapple, Cut-leaf Toothwort, Downy Yellow Violet, Bird's-foot Violet, Little Sweet Betsy, Large-flowered Trillium, Wild Columbine, Virginia Spiderwort, Pink Lady's-slipper, Yellow Lady's-slipper, Virginia Waterleaf, Yellow Stargrass, Blue-eyed Grass, Whorled Loosestrife, Canada Lily, Turk's-cap Lily, Spotted Jewelweed

Wisconsin (24)
Bloodroot, Trout Lily, Round-lobed Hepatica, Spring Beauty, Rue-anemone, Virginia Bluebell, Common Blue Violet, Twinleaf, Dutchman's Breeches, Wild Geranium, Showy Orchis, Mayapple, Cut-leaf Toothwort, Downy Yellow Violet, Bird's-foot Violet, Large-flowered Trillium, Wild Columbine, Pink Lady's-slipper, Yellow Lady's-slipper, Virginia Waterleaf, Yellow Stargrass, Blue-eyed Grass, Whorled Loosestrife, Spotted Jewelweed

Wyoming (2)
Downy Yellow Violet, Yellow Lady's-slipper

ISBN

Printed by